INTRODUCTION

What would Jesus do? Charles Sheldon based his novel *In His Steps* around that question. Today, we run into the same question everywhere; bracelets and pins and bumper stickers repeat the question again and again: WWJD?

Jesus Christ's life on earth changed the world forever for He showed us a radical new way to live. When we follow Him, we, too, will change the world. But how can we tell exactly what Jesus *would* do in any given situation?

This book answers that question with the actual accounts and sayings of Christ, along with other Scriptures. As you read, we hope you will be challenged—and comforted—by this Man's life-changing love.

WWJD

WWJD

compiled by
Ellyn Sanna

BARBOUR
PUBLISHING, INC.
Uhrichsville, Ohio

Published by Barbour Publishing, Inc., P.O. Box 719, Uhrichsville, Ohio 44683 http://www.barbourbooks.com

ecpa Member of the
Evangelical Christian
Publishers Association

Printed in the United States of America.

CONTENTS

HOW WOULD JESUS TREAT OTHERS?

"In everything,
do to others what you would
have them do to you,
for this sums up the Law
and the Prophets."

MATTHEW 7:12 NIV

WOULD JESUS
SHARE WHAT HE HAD
WITH OTHERS?

"Sell your possessions and give to the poor. Provide purses for yourselves that will not wear out, a treasure in heaven that will not be exhausted, where no thief comes near and no moth destroys. For where your treasure is, there will your heart will be also."

LUKE 12:33–34 NIV

"I tell you, use your worldly resources to benefit others and make friends. In this way, your generosity stores up a reward for you in heaven."

LUKE 16:9 NLT

Every man according as he purposeth in his heart, so let him give; not grudgingly, or of necessity: for God loveth a cheerful giver.

2 CORINTHIANS 9:7

He who gives to the poor will lack nothing.

PROVERBS 28:27 NIV

I have shewed you all things, how that so labouring ye ought to support the weak, and to remember the words of the Lord Jesus, how he said, "It is more blessed to give than to receive."

ACTS 20:35

Give all you have,
as well as you are,
a spiritual sacrifice to him
who withheld not from you
his Son, his only Son. . . .

JOHN WESLEY

Do not be hardhearted or tightfisted toward your poor brother.

DEUTERONOMY 15:7 NIV

If one of your countrymen becomes poor and is unable to support himself among you, help him . . .so he can continue to live among you.

LEVITICUS 25:35 NIV

A generous man will himself be blessed, for he shares his food with the poor.

PROVERBS 22:9 NIV

A generous man will prosper; he who refreshes others will himself be refreshed.

PROVERBS 11:25 NIV

———————————

How about the men who
possess large wealth?
Are they ready to take
that wealth and
use it as Jesus would?

IN HIS STEPS

———————————

Help me, Jesus, to share everything that You have given to me: my money, my possessions, my talents, my time, my love.

WHO WOULD JESUS INVITE FOR A MEAL?

Then said he also to him that bade him, "When thou makest a dinner or a supper, call not thy friends, nor thy brethren, neither thy kinsmen, nor thy rich neighbours; lest they also bid thee again, and a recompence be made thee. But when thou makest a feast, call the poor, the maimed, the lame, the blind: And thou shalt be blessed; for they cannot recompense thee: for thou shalt be recompensed at the resurrection of the just."

LUKE 14:12–14

You have been good to me. Somehow I feel as if it was what Jesus would do.

IN HIS STEPS

Lord, help me to be hospitable to all—not just to those I find attractive.

WOULD JESUS
BE PROUD?

Then Jesus came from Galilee to the Jordan to be baptized by John. But John tried to deter him, saying, "I need to be baptized by you, and do you come to me?"

Jesus replied, "Let it be so now. . . ." Then John consented.

MATTHEW 3:13–15 NIV

The pride of thine heart hath deceived thee, thou that dwellest in the clefts of the rock, whose habitation is high; that saith in his heart, Who shall bring me down to the ground?

OBADIAH 3

Now I Nebuchadnezzar praise and extol and honour the King of heaven, all whose works are truth, and his ways judgment: and those that walk in pride he is able to abase.

DANIEL 4:37

When pride comes, then comes disgrace, but with humility comes wisdom.

PROVERBS 11:2 NIV

If you are humble,
nothing will touch you,
neither praise nor disgrace,
because you know what you are.

MOTHER TERESA

The LORD shall cut off all flattering lips, and the tongue that speaketh proud things.

PSALM 12:3

God resisteth the proud, but giveth grace unto the humble.

JAMES 4:6

Lord, may I never consider myself more highly than I ought—nor too lowly. Help me to view myself and others the way you want me to.

WHAT WOULD JESUS DO IF
A SICK OR DISABLED
PERSON NEEDED HELP?

They brought unto him all sick people that were taken with divers diseases and torments, and those which were possessed with devils, and those which were lunatick, and those that had the palsy; and he healed them.

MATTHEW 4:24

And, behold, there came a leper and worshipped him, saying, "Lord, if thou wilt, thou canst make me clean." And Jesus put forth his hand, and touched him, saying, "I will; be thou clean." And immediately his leprosy was cleansed.

MATTHEW 8:2–3

Now when the sun was setting, all they that had any sick with divers diseases brought them unto him; and he laid his hands on every one of them, and healed them.

LUKE 4:40

And when Jesus was entered into Capernaum, there came unto him a centurion, beseeching him, And saying, "Lord, my servant lieth at home sick of the palsy, grievously tormented." And Jesus saith unto him, "I will come and heal him."

MATTHEW 8:5–7

O God,
Thou puttest into my heart
this great desire
to devote myself to
the sick and sorrowful.
I offer it to thee.
Give me my work to do.

FLORENCE NIGHTINGALE

And when Jesus was come into Peter's house, he saw his wife's mother laid, and sick of a fever. And he touched her hand, and the fever left her: and she arose, and ministered unto them.

MATTHEW 8:14–15

And, behold, they brought to him a man sick of the palsy, lying on a bed: and Jesus seeing their faith said unto the sick of the palsy; "Son, be of good cheer; thy sins be forgiven thee."

MATTHEW 9:2

And, behold, a woman, which was diseased with an issue of blood twelve years, came behind him, and touched the hem of his garment: For she said within herself, "If I may but touch his garment, I shall be whole." But Jesus turned him about, and when he saw her, he said, "Daughter, be of good comfort; thy faith hath made thee whole." And the woman was made whole from that hour. . . . And when Jesus departed thence, two blind men followed him, crying, and saying, "Thou son of David, have mercy on us." And when he was come into the house, the blind men came to him: and Jesus saith unto them, "Believe ye that I am able to do this?" They said unto him, "Yea, Lord." Then touched he their eyes, saying, "According to your faith be it unto you." And their eyes were opened.

MATTHEW 9:20–22, 27–30

And Jesus went about all the cities and villages, teaching in their synagogues, and preaching the gospel of the kingdom, and healing every sickness and every disease among the people.

MATTHEW 9:35

We need the eyes of deep faith
to see Christ in the broken body
and dirty clothes under which
the most beautiful One among
the sons of men hides.
We shall need the hands of Christ
to touch those bodies wounded
by pain and suffering. . . .
"What so ever you do to
the least of my brethren,
you do it unto me."

MOTHER TERESA

But when Jesus knew it, he withdrew himself from thence: and great multitudes followed him, and he healed them all.

MATTHEW 12:15

And Jesus went forth, and saw a great multitude, and was moved with compassion toward them, and he healed their sick.

MATTHEW 14:14

And there came a leper to him, beseeching him, and kneeling down to him, and saying unto him, "If thou wilt, thou canst make me clean." And Jesus, moved with compassion, put forth his hand, and touched him, and saith unto him, "I will; be thou clean."

MARK 1:40–41

There some people brought to him a man who was deaf and could hardly talk, and they begged him to place his hand on the man.

After he took him aside, away from the crowd, Jesus put his fingers into the man's ears. Then he spit and touched the man's tongue. He looked up to heaven and with a deep sigh said to him, "Eph-phatha!" (which means, "Be opened!"). At this, the man's ears were opened, his tongue was loosened and he began to speak plainly.

MARK 7:32–35 NIV

When they arrived at Bethsaida, some people brought a blind man to Jesus, and they begged him to touch and heal the man. Jesus took the blind man by the hand and led him out of the village. Then, spitting on the man's eyes, he laid his hands on him and asked, "Can you see anything now?"

The man looked around. "Yes," he said, "I see people, but I can't see them very clearly. They look like trees walking around."

Then Jesus placed his hands over the man's eyes again. As the man stared intently, his sight was completely restored, and he could see everything clearly.

MARK 8:22–25 NLT

And, behold, men brought in a bed a man which was taken with a palsy: and they sought means to bring him in, and to lay him before him. And when they could not find by what way they might bring him in because of the multitude, they went upon the housetop, and let him down through the tiling with his couch into the midst before Jesus. And when he saw their faith, he said unto him, "Man, thy sins are forgiven thee."

LUKE 5:18–20

And they came to Jericho: and as he went out of Jericho with his disciples and a great number of people, blind Bartimaeus, the son of Timaeus, sat by the highway side begging. And when he heard that it was Jesus of Nazareth, he began to cry out, and say, "Jesus, thou son of David, have mercy on me." And many charged him that he should hold his peace: but he cried the more a great deal, "Thou son of David, have mercy on me." And Jesus stood still, and commanded him to be called. And they call the blind man, saying unto him, "Be of good comfort, rise; he calleth thee." And he, casting away his garment, rose, and came to Jesus. And Jesus answered and said unto him, "What wilt thou that I should do unto thee?" The blind man said unto him, "Lord, that I might receive my sight." And Jesus said unto him, "Go thy way; thy faith hath made thee whole." And immediately he received his sight, and followed Jesus in the way.

MARK 10:46–52

Jesus, let me never forget that healing the sick and broken was such a large part of Your ministry. Remind me to take the time to reach out to those who are sick or in pain. Help me to see Your face in theirs.

WHAT WOULD JESUS SAY TO SOMEONE WHO DIDN'T BELIEVE IN ETERNAL LIFE?

"But in the account of the bush, even Moses showed that the dead rise, for he calls the Lord 'the God of Abraham, and the God of Isaac, and the God of Jacob.' He is not the God of the dead, but of the living, for to him all are alive."

LUKE 20:37–38 NIV

"Let not your heart be troubled: ye believe in God, believe also in me. In my Father's house are many mansions: if it were not so, I would have told you. I go to prepare a place for you. And if I go and prepare a place for you, I will come again, and receive you unto myself; that where I am, there ye may be also."

JOHN 14:1–3

"For God so loved the world, that he gave his only begotten Son, that whosoever believeth in him should not perish, but have everlasting life."

JOHN 3:16

And now, brothers and sisters, I want you to know what will happen to the Christians who have died so you will not be full of sorrow like people who have no hope. For since we believe that Jesus died and was raised to life again, we also believe that when Jesus comes, God will bring back with Jesus all the Christians who have died.

So comfort and encourage each other with these words.

1 THESSALONIANS 4:13–14, 18 NLT

You, bravest lion,
have burst through the heavens.
You have destroyed death,
and are building life in
the golden city.
Grant us society in that city,
and let us dwell in You.

HILDEGARD OF BINGEN

Lord, thank You for the eternal life that only You can provide.

HOW WOULD JESUS DO CHARITY WORK?

"Be careful not to do your 'acts of righteousness' before men, to be seen by them. If you do, you will have no reward from your Father in heaven.

"So when you give to the needy, do not announce it with trumpets, as the hypocrites do in the synagogues and on the streets, to be honored by men. I tell you the truth, they have received their reward in full. But when you give to the needy, do not let your left hand know what your right hand is doing, so that your giving may be in secret. Then your Father, who sees what is done in secret, will reward you."

MATTHEW 6:1–4 NIV

He that giveth, let him do it with simplicity.

ROMANS 12:8

For the poor shall never cease out of the land: therefore I command thee, saying, Thou shalt open thine hand wide unto thy brother, to thy poor, and to thy needy, in thy land.

DEUTERONOMY 15:11

"Give, and it shall be given unto you; good measure, pressed down, and shaken together, and running over, shall men give into your bosom. For with the same measure that ye mete withal it shall be measured to you again."

LUKE 6:38

Non-Christians and Christians
both do social work,
but non-Christians do it
for something while
we do it for Someone.

MOTHER TERESA

Jesus said unto him, "If thou wilt be perfect, go and sell that thou hast, and give to the poor, and thou shalt have treasure in heaven: and come and follow me."

MATTHEW 19:21

Fill me, Jesus, with Your love. Let me show that love to the world in concrete ways.

WHAT WOULD JESUS DO
IF SOMEONE HE KNEW WAS
DOING SOMETHING WRONG?

And the scribes and Pharisees brought unto him a woman taken in adultery; and when they had set her in the midst, They say unto him, "Master, this woman was taken in adultery, in the very act. Now Moses in the law commanded us, that such should be stoned: but what sayest thou?" This they said, tempting him, that they might have to accuse him. But Jesus stooped down, and with his finger wrote on the ground, as though he heard them not. So when they continued asking him, he lifted up himself, and said unto them, "He that is without sin among you, let him first cast a stone at her." And again he stooped down, and wrote on the ground. And they which heard it, being convicted by their own conscience, went out one by one, beginning at the eldest, even unto the last: and Jesus was left alone, and the woman standing in the midst. When Jesus had lifted up himself, and saw none but the woman, he said unto her, "Woman, where are those thine accusers? hath no man condemned thee?" She said, "No man, Lord."

And Jesus said unto her, "Neither do I condemn thee: go, and sin no more."

JOHN 8:3–11

"Judge not, that ye be not judged. For with what judgment ye judge, ye shall be judged: and with what measure ye mete, it shall be measured to you again. And why beholdest thou the mote that is in thy brother's eye, but considerest not the beam that is in thine own eye? Or how wilt thou say to thy brother, Let me pull out the mote out of thine eye; and, behold, a beam is in thine own eye? Thou hypocrite, first cast out the beam out of thine own eye; and then shalt thou see clearly to cast out the mote out of thy brother's eye."

MATTHEW 7:1–5

"Judge not, and ye shall not be judged: condemn not, and ye shall not be condemned: forgive, and ye shall be forgiven."

LUKE 6:37

Forgive me for the times I've judged others, Lord. Help me to pray for them instead, while I concentrate on keeping my own behavior in line with Your love.

WOULD JESUS
SPEND TIME WITH SINNERS?

Then drew near unto him all the publicans and sinners for to hear him. And the Pharisees and scribes murmured, saying, "This man receiveth sinners, and eateth with them."

LUKE 15:1–2

Who were these people?
They were immortal souls.
What was Christianity?
A calling of sinners,
not the righteous,
to repentance.

IN HIS STEPS

"Verily I say unto you, That the publicans and the harlots go into the kingdom of God before you."

MATTHEW 21:31

And it came to pass, as Jesus sat at meat in the house, behold, many publicans and sinners came and sat down with him and his disciples. And when the Pharisees saw it, they said unto his disciples, "Why eateth your Master with publicans and sinners?" But when Jesus heard that, he said unto them, "They that be whole need not a physician, but they that are sick. But go ye and learn what that meaneth, I will have mercy, and not sacrifice: for I am not come to call the righteous, but sinners to repentance."

MATTHEW 9:10–13

We are a long way
from following in the steps
of Him who trod the way
with groans and tears
and sobs of anguish
for lost humanity.

IN HIS STEPS

"Joy shall be in heaven over one sinner that repenteth."

LUKE 15:7

And, behold, a woman in the city, which was a sinner, when she knew that Jesus sat at meat in the Pharisee's house, brought an alabaster box of ointment, And stood at his feet behind him weeping, and began to wash his feet with tears, and did wipe them with the hairs of her head, and kissed his feet, and anointed them with the ointment.

LUKE 7:37–38

"The Son of man came eating and drinking, and they say, Behold a man gluttonous, and a winebibber, a friend of publicans and sinners. But wisdom is justified of her children."

MATTHEW 11:19

Help me, God, not to hold myself apart from others, thinking I'm better than they. Remind me that You loved us enough to send Your Son to live among us—and give me that same love for others.

WOULD JESUS
CELEBRATE WITH
OTHERS' JOY?

And the third day there was a marriage in Cana of Galilee; and the mother of Jesus was there: And both Jesus was called, and his disciples, to the marriage.

JOHN 2:1–2

Rejoice with them that do rejoice.

ROMANS 12:15

I am glad and rejoice with all of you. So you too should be glad and rejoice with me.

PHILIPPIANS 2:17–18 NIV

Thank You, Lord, that You celebrated and rejoiced with Your friends. When I am having a good time with my own friends, please be at the center of our pleasure.

Would Jesus spend time with His closest friends, depending on them for emotional support?

And he took with him Peter and the two sons of Zebedee, and began to be sorrowful and very heavy. Then saith he unto them, "My soul is exceeding sorrowful, even unto death: tarry ye here, and watch with me."

Matthew 26:37–38

Then Peter, turning about, seeth the disciple whom Jesus loved following; which also leaned on his breast at supper.

John 21:20

And after six days Jesus taketh with him Peter, and James, and John, and leadeth them up into an high mountain apart by themselves.

Mark 9:2

A man that hath friends must shew himself friendly: and there is a friend that sticketh closer than a brother.

PROVERBS 18:24

If I shall,
in the course of my
obedience to my promise,
meet with loss or
trouble in the world,
I can depend upon the genuine,
practical sympathy and fellowship
of any other Christian who has,
with me, made the pledge to do
all things by the rule,
"What would Jesus do?"

IN HIS STEPS

Faithful are the wounds of a friend; but the kisses of an enemy are deceitful. . . . Ointment and perfume rejoice the heart: so doth the sweetness of a man's friend by hearty counsel. . . . Iron sharpeneth iron; so a man sharpeneth the countenance of his friend.

PROVERBS 27:6, 9, 17

A friend loveth at all times, and a brother is born for adversity.

PROVERBS 17:17

Then said the Jews, Behold how he loved him!

JOHN 11:36

Thank You for my friends, Lord. May our friendship with each other bring us closer to You.

HOW WOULD JESUS
TREAT CHILDREN?

But when the chief priests and the teachers of the law saw the wonderful things he did and the children shouting in the temple area, "Hosanna to the Son of David," they were indignant.

"Do you hear what these children are saying?" they asked him.

"Yes," replied Jesus, "have you never read, " 'From the lips of children and infants you have ordained praise'?"

MATTHEW 21:15–16 NIV

One day some parents brought their little children to Jesus so he could touch them and bless them, but the disciples told them not to bother him. Then Jesus called for the children and said to the disciples, "Let the children come to me. Don't stop them! For the Kingdom of God belongs to such as these. I assure you, anyone who doesn't have their kind of faith will never get into the Kingdom of God."

LUKE 18:15–17 NLT

At the same time came the disciples unto Jesus, saying, "Who is the greatest in the kingdom of heaven?" . . . "Verily I say unto you, Except ye be converted, and become as little children, ye shall not enter into the kingdom of heaven. Whosoever therefore shall humble himself as this little child, the same is greatest in the kingdom of heaven. And whoso shall receive one such little child in my name receiveth me. But whoso shall offend one of these little ones which believe in me, it were better for him that a millstone were hanged about his neck, and that he were drowned in the depth of the sea."

MATTHEW 18:1, 3–6

Then were there brought unto him little children, that he should put his hands on them, and pray: and the disciples rebuked them. But Jesus said, "Suffer little children, and forbid them not, to come unto me: for of such is the kingdom of heaven." And he laid his hands on them.

MATTHEW 19:13–15

"Take heed that ye despise not one of these little ones; for I say unto you, That in heaven their angels do always behold the face of my Father which is in heaven."

MATTHEW 18:10

"O Jerusalem, Jerusalem, which killest the prophets, and stonest them that are sent unto thee; how often would I have gathered thy children together, as a hen doth gather her brood under her wings, and ye would not!"

Endeavor to
become as
humble and simple
as a little child
for the love
of our Lord,
in imitation of him.

JEAN-PIERRE DE CAUSSADE

Remind me, Jesus, that when I take time for children I am also taking time for You.

WHAT WOULD JESUS DO IF SOMEONE ASKED HIM FOR HELP?

And, behold, there came a leper and worshipped him, saying, "Lord, if thou wilt, thou canst make me clean." And Jesus put forth his hand, and touched him, saying, "I will; be thou clean." And immediately his leprosy was cleansed.

MATTHEW 8:2–3

And immediately Jesus stretched forth his hand, and caught him.

MATTHEW 14:31

Lord, remind me that You enjoy my prayers—even the times I'm asking You for help. May I never forget Your words, as recorded in the Book of Matthew, "What man is there of you, whom if his son ask bread, will he give him a stone? Or if he ask a fish, will he give him a serpent? If ye then, being evil, know how to give good gifts unto your children, how much more shall your Father which is in heaven give good things to them that ask him?"

Would Jesus put His family's wishes first, ahead of His relationship with God?

While he yet talked to the people, behold, his mother and his brethren stood without, desiring to speak with him. Then one said unto him, "Behold, thy mother and thy brethren stand without, desiring to speak with thee." But he answered and said unto him that told him, "Who is my mother? and who are my brethren?" And he stretched forth his hand toward his disciples, and said, "Behold my mother and my brethren! For whosoever shall do the will of my Father which is in heaven, the same is my brother, and sister, and mother."

MATTHEW 12:46–50

"If you want to be my follower you must love me more than your own father and mother, wife and children, brothers and sisters—yes, more than your own life."

LUKE 14:26 NLT

"Think not that I am come to send peace on earth: I came not to send peace, but a sword. For I am come to set a man at variance against his father, and the daughter against her mother, and the daughter in law against her mother in law. And a man's foes shall be they of his own household. He that loveth father or mother more than me is not worthy of me: and he that loveth son or daughter more than me is not worthy of me."

MATTHEW 10:34–37

Truly, a man's foes are
they of his own household
when the rule of Jesus is
obeyed by some and
disobeyed by others.
Jesus is a
great divider of life.
One must walk
parallel with Him
or directly across His way.

IN HIS STEPS

And when they saw him, they were amazed: and his mother said unto him, "Son, why hast thou thus dealt with us? behold, thy father and I have sought thee sorrowing." And he said unto them, "How is it that ye sought me? wist ye not that I must be about my Father's business?"

LUKE 2:48–49

And he said unto them, "Verily I say unto you, There is no man that hath left house, or parents, or brethren, or wife, or children, for the kingdom of God's sake, Who shall not receive manifold more in this present time, and in the world to come life everlasting."

LUKE 18:29–30

Let me follow You, my Lord, no matter what my family thinks, whether they approve or disapprove.

WOULD JESUS WORRY MORE ABOUT PRACTICAL CONCERNS THAN PEOPLE'S FEELINGS?

There came unto him a woman having an alabaster box of very precious ointment, and poured it on his head, as he sat at meat. But when his disciples saw it, they had indignation, saying, "To what purpose is this waste? For this ointment might have been sold for much, and given to the poor." When Jesus understood it, he said unto them, "Why trouble ye the woman? for she hath wrought a good work upon me."

MATTHEW 26:7–10

Lord, I don't always understand other peoples' actions—but You do. Help me not to criticize others, Lord, but to be as concerned about their feelings as I am about mine. May I always act as You would act, and always point others to You.

WOULD JESUS THINK
SOME KIND ACTS TOO TRIVIAL
TO WORRY ABOUT?

"For I was an hungered, and ye gave me meat: I was thirsty, and ye gave me drink: I was a stranger, and ye took me in: Naked, and ye clothed me: I was sick, and ye visited me: I was in prison, and ye came unto me. Then shall the righteous answer him, saying, Lord, when saw we thee an hungered, and fed thee? or thirsty, and gave thee drink? When saw we thee a stranger, and took thee in? or naked, and clothed thee? Or when saw we thee sick, or in prison, and came unto thee? And the King shall answer and say unto them, Verily I say unto you, Inasmuch as ye have done it unto one of the least of these my brethren, ye have done it unto me."

MATTHEW 25:35–40

"And whosoever shall give to drink unto one of these little ones a cup of cold water only in the name of a disciple, verily I say unto you, he shall in no wise lose his reward."

MATTHEW 10:42

Jesus knew that the Father had put all things under his power, and that he had come from God and was returning to God; so he got up from the meal, took off his outer clothing, and wrapped a towel around his waist. After that, he poured water into a basin and began to wash his disciples' feet, drying them with the towel that was wrapped around him.

JOHN 13:3–5 NIV

I will let no
tiny sacrifice pass. . . .
I wish to profit by
the smallest actions
and to do them for love.

THERESE OF LISIEUX

Lord, I ask that You fill even the smallest of my acts with Your love.

Love is never abstract.
It does not adhere to the
universe or the planet or
the nation or the institution
or the profession,
but to the singularity of
the sparrows of the street,
the lilies of the field,
"the least of these my brethren."
Love. . .exists by its
willingness to be anonymous,
humble, and unrewarded.

WENDELL BERRY

HOW WOULD JESUS TREAT
A PERSON WHO IS
MENTALLY ILL?

And when they were come to the multitude, there came to him a certain man, kneeling down to him, and saying, "Lord, have mercy on my son: for he is a lunatick, and sore vexed: for ofttimes he falleth into the fire, and oft into the water. . . ." And Jesus rebuked the devil; and he departed out of him: and the child was cured from that very hour.

MATTHEW 17:14–15, 18

And when he was come into the ship, he that had been possessed with the devil prayed him that he might be with him. Howbeit Jesus suffered him not, but saith unto him, "Go home to thy friends, and tell them how great things the Lord hath done for thee, and hath had compassion on thee."

MARK 5:18–19

Lord, may I always respond with compassion to those who suffer from a mental illness.

What would Jesus do if He were faced with a group of hungry people?

And when it was evening, his disciples came to him, saying, "This is a desert place, and the time is now past; send the multitude away, that they may go into the villages, and buy themselves victuals." But Jesus said unto them, "They need not depart; give ye them to eat." And they say unto him, "We have here but five loaves, and two fishes." He said, "Bring them hither to me." And he commanded the multitude to sit down on the grass, and took the five loaves, and the two fishes, and looking up to heaven, he blessed, and brake, and gave the loaves to his disciples, and the disciples to the multitude. And they did all eat, and were filled: and they took up of the fragments that remained twelve baskets full. And they that had eaten were about five thousand men, beside women and children.

MATTHEW 14:15–21

And Jesus, when he came out, saw much people, and was moved with compassion toward them, because they were as sheep not having a shepherd: and he began to teach them many things. And when the day was now far spent, his disciples came unto him, and said, "This is a desert place, and now the time is far passed: Send them away, that they may go into the country round about, and into the villages, and buy themselves bread: for they have nothing to eat." He answered and said unto them, "Give ye them to eat."

MARK 6:34–37

Then Jesus called his disciples unto him, and said, "I have compassion on the multitude, because they continue with me now three days, and have nothing to eat: and I will not send them away fasting, lest they faint in the way."

MATTHEW 15:32

Help me to remember, Lord, that something as ordinary as preparing a meal can be opportunity for Your grace to shine.

WOULD JESUS ARGUE
AND PRESENT HIS
OPINIONS LOUDLY?

He shall not strive, nor cry; neither shall any man hear his voice in the streets.

MATTHEW 12:19

The place of the scripture which he read was this, "He was led as a sheep to the slaughter; and like a lamb dumb before his shearer, so opened he not his mouth."

ACTS 8:32

And Pilate asked him again, saying, "Answerest thou nothing? behold how many things they witness against thee." But Jesus yet answered nothing; so that Pilate marvelled.

MARK 15:4–5

I don't always need to be heard or understood by others, Lord. Help me to realize that You hear and understand me—and that's what is most important.

How would Jesus react to a selfish person who was not willing to help others?

Then Jesus beholding him loved him, and said unto him, "One thing thou lackest: go thy way, sell whatsoever thou hast, and give to the poor, and thou shalt have treasure in heaven: and come, take up the cross, and follow me."

MARK 10:21

Do nothing out of selfish ambition or vain conceit, but in humility consider others better than yourselves.

PHILIPPIANS 2:3 NIV

Thank You, Lord, that You loved the selfish rich man; thank You that You love me even when I put myself ahead of others. Teach me to be more like You. Show me how to share all that You have given me.

HOW WOULD JESUS JUDGE PEOPLE— BY THEIR MONEY OR BY THEIR LOVE?

And there came a certain poor widow, and she threw in two mites, which make a farthing. And he called unto him his disciples, and saith unto them, "Verily I say unto you, That this poor widow hath cast more in, than all they which have cast into the treasury: For all they did cast in of their abundance; but she of her want did cast in all that she had, even all her living."

MARK 12:42–44

If we do not cling to riches, selfishness, or greed— then I believe we are getting closer to God.

DANIEL ORTEGA

Wealth is nothing compared to love, Lord. May my priorities always be correct and true.

WOULD JESUS CARE ABOUT POOR PEOPLE?

"The Spirit of the Lord is upon me, because he hath anointed me to preach the gospel to the poor."

LUKE 4:18

Jesus answered and said unto them, "Go and shew John again those things which ye do hear and see: The blind receive their sight, and the lame walk, the lepers are cleansed, and the deaf hear, the dead are raised up, and the poor have the gospel preached to them."

MATTHEW 11:4–5

Jesus said unto him, "If thou wilt be perfect, go and sell that thou hast, and give to the poor, and thou shalt have treasure in heaven: and come and follow me."

MATTHEW 19:21

Lord, You said that we would always have poor people in our society. Help me to love them as You do.

WOULD JESUS CARE ABOUT PEOPLE WHO WERE EMOTIONALLY AS WELL AS PHYSICALLY HURT?

And he said unto them, "What manner of communications are these that ye have one to another, as ye walk, and are sad?"

LUKE 24:17

"He hath sent me to heal the brokenhearted. . .to set at liberty them that are bruised."

LUKE 4:18

"Verily, verily, I say unto you, That ye shall weep and lament, but the world shall rejoice: and ye shall be sorrowful, but your sorrow shall be turned into joy."

JOHN 16:20

Lord, You cared about the emotional needs of Your disciples and the others around You. May I be as concerned about the people around me.

HOW WOULD JESUS RELATE TO GOD?

"I have glorified thee on the earth:
I have finished the work
which thou gavest me to do.
And now, O Father,
glorify thou me with thine own self
with the glory which I had
with thee before the world was."

JOHN 17:4–5

How would Jesus pray?

"And when thou prayest, thou shalt not be as the hypocrites are: for they love to pray standing in the synagogues and in the corners of the streets, that they may be seen of men. Verily I say unto you, They have their reward. But thou, when thou prayest, enter into thy closet, and when thou hast shut thy door, pray to thy Father which is in secret; and thy Father which seeth in secret shall reward thee openly. But when ye pray, use not vain repetitions, as the heathen do: for they think that they shall be heard for their much speaking. Be not ye therefore like unto them: for your Father knoweth what things ye have need of, before ye ask him. After this manner therefore pray ye: Our Father which art in heaven, Hallowed be thy name. Thy kingdom come. Thy will be done in earth, as it is in heaven. Give us this day our daily bread. And forgive us our debts, as we forgive our debtors. And lead us not into temptation, but deliver us from evil: For thine is the kingdom, and the power, and the glory, for ever. Amen."

MATTHEW 6:5–13

And Jesus answering saith unto them, "Have faith in God. For verily I say unto you, That whosoever shall say unto this mountain, Be thou removed, and be thou cast into the sea; and shall not doubt in his heart, but shall believe that those things which he saith shall come to pass; he shall have whatsoever he saith. Therefore I say unto you, What things soever ye desire, when ye pray, believe that ye receive them, and ye shall have them.

"And when ye stand praying, forgive, if ye have ought against any: that your Father also which is in heaven may forgive you your trespasses. But if ye do not forgive, neither will your Father which is in heaven forgive your trespasses."

MARK 11:22–26

"Ask, and it shall be given you; seek, and ye shall find; knock, and it shall be opened unto you: For every one that asketh receiveth; and he that seeketh findeth; and to him that knocketh it shall be opened. Or what man is there of you, whom if his son ask bread, will he give him a stone? Or if he ask a fish, will he give him a serpent? If ye then, being evil, know how to give good gifts unto your children, how much more shall your Father which is in heaven give good things to them that ask him?"

MATTHEW 7:7–11

Jesus answered and said unto them, "Verily I say unto you, If ye have faith, and doubt not. . .ye shall say unto this mountain, Be thou removed, and be thou cast into the sea; it shall be done. And all things, whatsoever ye shall ask in prayer, believing, ye shall receive."

MATTHEW 21:21–22

```
      I believe that we get
  an answer to our prayers when
  we are willing to obey what is
      implicit in that answer.
 I believe we get a vision of God
     when we are willing to
     accept what that vision
            does to us.
```

ELSIE CHAMBERLAIN

My voice shalt thou hear in the morning, O LORD; in the morning will I direct my prayer unto thee, and will look up.

PSALM 5:3

Be careful for nothing; but in every thing by prayer and supplication with thanksgiving let your requests be made known unto God.

PHILIPPIANS 4:6

Is any among you afflicted? let him pray.

JAMES 5:13

Prayer is nothing else,
in my opinion,
but friendly conversation,
frequently conversing alone,
with One who we know
loves us.

TERESA OF AVILA

Defraud ye not one the other, except it be with consent for a time, that ye may give yourselves to fasting and prayer; and come together again, that Satan tempt you not for your incontinency.

1 CORINTHIANS 7:5

Likewise the Spirit also helpeth our infirmities: for we know not what we should pray for as we ought: but the Spirit itself maketh intercession for us with groanings which cannot be uttered.

ROMANS 8:26

Pray without ceasing.

1 THESSALONIANS 5:17

Remote from man,
with God he passed the days;
Prayer all his business,
all his pleasure praise.

THOMAS PARNELL

Pray one for another, that ye may be healed. The effectual fervent prayer of a righteous man availeth much.

JAMES 5:16

Help me, Jesus, to always be open to Your Spirit, so that the lines of communication between us are never closed.

WOULD JESUS
READ THE BIBLE?

He went to Nazareth, where he had been brought up, and on the Sabbath day he went into the synagogue, as was his custom. And he stood up to read. The scroll of the prophet Isaiah was handed to him. Unrolling it, he found the place where it is written: "The Spirit of the Lord is on me, because he has anointed me to preach good news to the poor. He has sent me to proclaim freedom for the prisoners and recovery of sight for the blind, to release the oppressed, to proclaim the year of the Lord's favor." Then he rolled up the scroll, gave it back to the attendant and sat down. The eyes of everyone in the synagogue were fastened on him, and he began by saying to them, "Today this scripture is fulfilled in your hearing."

LUKE 4:16–21 NIV

"Search the scriptures; for in them ye think ye have eternal life: and they are they which testify of me."

JOHN 5:39

Thy word is a lamp unto my feet, and a light unto my path.

PSALM 119:105

Don't worry about
what you don't understand
(in the Bible). . . .
Worry about what
you do understand
but do not live by.

CORRIE TEN BOOM

All scripture is given by inspiration of God, and is profitable for doctrine, for reproof, for correction, for instruction in righteousness.

2 TIMOTHY 3:16

Your Word is my road map, instruction manual, and love letter, Father. May I be like Jesus, who studied and understood the Scriptures.

WOULD JESUS TALK ABOUT HIMSELF MORE THAN HIS HEAVENLY FATHER?

"He that speaketh of himself seeketh his own glory: but he that seeketh his glory that sent him, the same is true, and no unrighteousness is in him."

JOHN 7:18

Then cried Jesus in the temple as he taught, saying, "Ye both know me, and ye know whence I am: and I am not come of myself, but he that sent me is true, whom ye know not."

JOHN 7:28

Then said Jesus unto them, "When ye have lifted up the Son of man, then shall ye know that I am he, and that I do nothing of myself; but as my Father hath taught me, I speak these things."

JOHN 8:28

"And I seek not mine own glory: there is one that seeketh and judgeth."

JOHN 8:50

"My Father. . .is greater than all."

JOHN 10:29

"Ye have heard how I said unto you, I go away, and come again unto you. If ye loved me, ye would rejoice, because I said, I go unto the Father: for my Father is greater than I."

JOHN 14:28

"All things are delivered unto me of my Father."

MATTHEW 11:27

"This commandment have I received of my Father."

JOHN 10:18

Help me, God, to talk about You more than I do myself.

WHAT WOULD JESUS SAY WAS THE ONLY WAY TO ETERNAL LIFE?

And, behold, a certain lawyer stood up, and tempted him, saying, "Master, what shall I do to inherit eternal life?" He said unto him, "What is written in the law? how readest thou?" And he answering said, "Thou shalt love the Lord thy God with all thy heart, and with all thy soul, and with all thy strength, and with all thy mind; and thy neighbour as thyself." And he said unto him, "Thou hast answered right: this do, and thou shalt live."

LUKE 10:25–28

Jesus saith unto him, "I am the way, the truth, and the life: no man cometh unto the Father, but by me."

JOHN 14:6

"For the Son of man is come to seek and to save that which was lost."

LUKE 19:10

Neither is there salvation in any other: for there is none other name under heaven given among men, whereby we must be saved.

ACTS 4:12

For I am not ashamed of the gospel of Christ: for it is the power of God unto salvation to every one that believeth; to the Jew first, and also to the Greek.

ROMANS 1:16

And you also were included in Christ when you heard the word of truth, the gospel of your salvation. Having believed, you were marked in him with a seal, the promised Holy Spirit, who is a deposit guaranteeing our inheritance until the redemption of those who are God's possession— to the praise of his glory.

EPHESIANS 1:13–14 NIV

We're playing "Follow the Leader," Lord. You lead, I'll follow—all the way to eternity.

HOW WOULD JESUS HANDLE TROUBLE AND TEMPTATION?

"And whosoever doth not bear his cross,
and come after me,
cannot be my disciple."

LUKE 14:27

WHAT WOULD JESUS DO IF HE WERE TEMPTED TO PUT HIS PHYSICAL NEEDS AHEAD OF HIS SPIRITUAL ONES?

From that time forth began Jesus to shew unto his disciples, how that he must go unto Jerusalem, and suffer many things of the elders and chief priests and scribes, and be killed, and be raised again the third day. Then Peter took him, and began to rebuke him, saying, "Be it far from thee, Lord: this shall not be unto thee." But he turned, and said unto Peter, "Get thee behind me, Satan: thou art an offence unto me: for thou savourest not the things that be of God, but those that be of men." Then said Jesus unto his disciples, "If any man will come after me, let him deny himself, and take up his cross, and follow me. For whosoever will save his life shall lose it: and whosoever will lose his life for my sake shall find it. For what is a man profited, if he shall gain the whole world, and lose his own soul? or what shall a man give in exchange for his soul?"

MATTHEW 16:21–26

And when he had fasted forty days and forty nights, he was afterward an hungered. And when the tempter came to him, he said, "If thou be the Son of God, command that these stones be made bread." But he answered and said, "It is written, Man shall not live by bread alone, but by every word that proceedeth out of the mouth of God."

MATTHEW 4:2–4

Our Christianity loves its ease
and comfort too well to take up
anything so rough
and heavy as a cross.

IN HIS STEPS

"And if thy right eye offend thee, pluck it out, and cast it from thee: for it is profitable for thee that one of thy members should perish, and not that thy whole body should be cast into hell. And if thy right hand offend thee, cut it off, and cast it from thee: for it is profitable for thee that one of thy members should perish, and not that thy whole body should be cast into hell."

MATTHEW 5:29–30

"Wherefore if thy hand or thy foot offend thee, cut them off, and cast them from thee: it is better for thee to enter into life halt or maimed, rather than having two hands or two feet to be cast into everlasting fire. And if thine eye offend thee, pluck it out, and cast it from thee: it is better for thee to enter into life with one eye, rather than having two eyes to be cast into hell fire."

MATTHEW 18:8–9

Flee also youthful lusts: but follow righteousness, faith, charity, peace, with them that call on the Lord out of a pure heart.

2 TIMOTHY 2:22

Help me, Father, not to love my comfort more than I love You.

WHAT WOULD JESUS DO
IF HE WERE TEMPTED TO
CRAVE POWER AND PRESTIGE?

Again, the devil taketh him up into an exceeding high mountain, and sheweth him all the kingdoms of the world, and the glory of them; And saith unto him, "All these things will I give thee, if thou wilt fall down and worship me." Then saith Jesus unto him, "Get thee hence, Satan: for it is written, Thou shalt worship the Lord thy God, and him only shalt thou serve." Then the devil leaveth him, and, behold, angels came and ministered unto him.

MATTHEW 4:8–11

And he opened his mouth, and taught them, saying, "Blessed are the poor in spirit: for theirs is the kingdom of heaven."

MATTHEW 5:2–3

Better it is to be of an humble spirit with the lowly, than to divide the spoil with the proud.

PROVERBS 16:19

He hath shewed thee, O man, what is good; and what doth the LORD require of thee, but to do justly, and to love mercy, and to walk humbly with thy God?

MICAH 6:8

"What would Jesus do?"
Felicia prayed and hoped and
worked and regulated her life
by the answer to that question.
It was the inspiration of
her conduct and
the answer to her ambition.

IN HIS STEPS

A man's pride shall bring him low: but honour shall uphold the humble in spirit.

PROVERBS 29:23

Pride only breeds quarrels.

PROVERBS 13:10 NIV

Pride goes before destruction, a haughty spirit before a fall. Better to be lowly in spirit and among the oppressed than to share plunder with the proud.

PROVERBS 16:18–19 NIV

But he giveth more grace. Wherefore he saith, God resisteth the proud, but giveth grace unto the humble.

JAMES 4:6

Put on therefore, as the elect of God, holy and beloved, bowels of mercies, kindness, humbleness of mind, meekness, longsuffering.

COLOSSIANS 3:12

The meek will he guide in judgment: and the meek will he teach his way.

PSALM 25:9

May Your love, Christ, regulate my life.

WOULD JESUS
EVER AVOID TROUBLE?

"But when they persecute you in this city, flee ye into another."

MATTHEW 10:23

Then the Pharisees went out, and held a council against him, how they might destroy him. But when Jesus knew it, he withdrew himself from thence.

MATTHEW 12:14–15

And when they were departed, behold, the angel of the Lord appeareth to Joseph in a dream, saying, Arise, and take the young child and his mother, and flee into Egypt, and be thou there until I bring thee word: for Herod will seek the young child to destroy him.

MATTHEW 2:13

Give me wisdom, Jesus, to know when to run from trouble—but always toward You.

WHAT WOULD JESUS SAY TO SOMEONE WHO WAS FRUSTRATED BY THE CARES OF EVERYDAY LIFE?

But Martha was cumbered about much serving, and came to him, and said, "Lord, dost thou not care that my sister hath left me to serve alone? bid her therefore that she help me." And Jesus answered and said unto her, "Martha, Martha, thou art careful and troubled about many things: But one thing is needful; and Mary hath chosen that good part, which shall not be taken away from her."

LUKE 10:40–42

"Abide in me, and I in you. As the branch cannot bear fruit of itself, except it abide in the vine; no more can ye, except ye abide in me. . . . If ye keep my commandments, ye shall abide in my love; even as I have kept my Father's commandments, and abide in his love. These things have I spoken unto you, that my joy might remain in you, and that your joy might be full."

JOHN 15:4, 10–11

"Let not your heart be troubled: ye believe in God, believe also in me. In my Father's house are many mansions: if it were not so, I would have told you. I go to prepare a place for you. And if I go and prepare a place for you, I will come again, and receive you unto myself; that where I am, there ye may be also."

JOHN 14:1–3

We need. . .
only a heart determined
to devote itself to
nothing except Him,
for Him, loving Him only.

BROTHER LAWRENCE

Blessed be God, even the Father of our Lord Jesus Christ, the Father of mercies, and the God of all comfort; Who comforteth us in all our tribulation, that we may be able to comfort them which are in any trouble, by the comfort wherewith we ourselves are comforted of God.

2 CORINTHIANS 1:3–4

Casting all your care upon him; for he careth for you.

1 PETER 5:7

For whatsoever things were written aforetime were written for our learning, that we through patience and comfort of the scriptures might have hope.

ROMANS 15:4

When life seems overwhelming, Lord, remind me to abide in You, relying on You for strength. Help me to focus on You rather than on my work, for You are the "one thing" that is "needful." And when I see others around me who are obviously hassled and frustrated, let me remember to reach out to them with Your love and understanding.

WOULD JESUS USE VIOLENCE TO DEFEND HIMSELF?

Then said Jesus unto him, "Put up again thy sword into his place: for all they that take the sword shall perish with the sword."

MATTHEW 26:52

A violent man enticeth his neighbour, and leadeth him into the way that is not good.

PROVERBS 16:29

Do violence to no man, neither accuse any falsely; and be content with your wages.

LUKE 3:14

The LORD trieth the righteous: but the wicked and him that loveth violence his soul hateth.

PSALM 11:5

Lord, I live in a violent society. May I never add to that violence.

WHAT WOULD JESUS SAY
IF HE WERE ABANDONED
BY HIS FRIENDS?

"The time is coming—in fact, it is already here—when you will be scattered, each one going his own way, leaving me alone. Yet I am not alone because the Father is with me."

JOHN 16:32 NLT

Trust ye not in a friend, put ye not confidence in a guide: keep the doors of thy mouth from her that lieth in thy bosom. . . . Therefore I will look unto the LORD; I will wait for the God of my salvation: my God will hear me.

MICAH 7:5, 7

Even when others turn their backs on me, thank You, Lord, that You are still with me.

WOULD JESUS TAKE REVENGE AGAINST SOMEONE WHO WAS UNKIND TO HIM?

"And as ye would that men should do to you, do ye also to them likewise. For if ye love them which love you, what thank have ye? for sinners also love those that love them. And if ye do good to them which do good to you, what thank have ye? for sinners also do even the same. And if ye lend to them of whom ye hope to receive, what thank have ye? for sinners also lend to sinners, to receive as much again. But love ye your enemies, and do good, and lend, hoping for nothing again; and your reward shall be great, and ye shall be the children of the Highest: for he is kind unto the unthankful and to the evil. Be ye therefore merciful, as your Father also is merciful. Judge not, and ye shall not be judged: condemn not, and ye shall not be condemned: forgive, and ye shall be forgiven."

LUKE 6:31–37

Why should God lose you?
It is a great thing to win
the love of the Great Father.
It is a small thing that
I should love you.
But if you need to feel again
that there is love in the world,
you will believe me when I say,
my brothers, that I love you,
and in the name of Him who
was crucified for our sins
I cannot bear to see you miss
the glory of the human life. . . .
No one but God and
you and myself need ever know
anything of this tonight.
He has forgiven it
the minute you ask Him to.

In His Steps

And when his disciples James and John saw this, they said, "Lord, wilt thou that we command fire to come down from heaven, and consume them, even as Elias did?" But he turned, and rebuked them, and said, "Ye know not what manner of spirit ye are of. For the Son of man is not come to destroy men's lives, but to save them." And they went to another village.

LUKE 9:54–56

"And forgive us our sins; for we also forgive every one that is indebted to us."

LUKE 11:4

"Take heed to yourselves: If thy brother trespass against thee, rebuke him; and if he repent, forgive him. And if he trespass against thee seven times in a day, and seven times in a day turn again to thee, saying, I repent; thou shalt forgive him."

LUKE 17:3–4

Then said Jesus, "Father, forgive them; for they know not what they do." And they parted his raiment, and cast lots.

LUKE 23:34

"Ye have heard that it hath been said, An eye for an eye, and a tooth for a tooth: But I say unto you, That ye resist not evil: but whosoever shall smite thee on thy right cheek, turn to him the other also. . . . Ye have heard that it hath been said, Thou shalt love thy neighbour, and hate thine enemy. But I say unto you, Love your enemies, bless them that curse you, do good to them that hate you, and pray for them which despitefully use you, and persecute you; That ye may be the children of your Father which is in heaven: for he maketh his sun to rise on the evil and on the good, and sendeth rain on the just and on the unjust. For if ye love them which love you, what reward have ye? do not even the publicans the same? And if ye salute your brethren only, what do ye more than others? do not even the publicans so? Be ye therefore perfect, even as your Father which is in heaven is perfect."

MATTHEW 5:38–39, 43–48

"For if ye forgive men their trespasses, your heavenly Father will also forgive you: But if ye forgive not men their trespasses, neither will your Father forgive your trespasses."

MATTHEW 6:14–15

"Moreover if thy brother shall trespass against thee, go and tell him his fault between thee and him alone: if he shall hear thee, thou hast gained thy brother. But if he will not hear thee, then take with thee one or two more, that in the mouth of two or three witnesses every word may be established. And if he shall neglect to hear them, tell it unto the church: but if he neglect to hear the church, let him be unto thee as an heathen man and a publican. . . ."

Then came Peter to him, and said, Lord, how oft shall my brother sin against me, and I forgive him? till seven times? Jesus saith unto him, "I say not unto thee, Until seven times: but, Until seventy times seven."

MATTHEW 18:15–17, 21–22

Do not repay anyone evil for evil. . . . Do not take revenge, my friends. . . . On the contrary: "If your enemy is hungry, feed him; if he is thirsty, give him something to drink. In doing this, you will heap burning coals on his head." Do not be overcome by evil, but overcome evil with good.

ROMANS 12:17, 19, 20–21 NIV

Help me, Christ, to forgive those who have hurt me. Remind me of all the things for which You have forgiven me. Fill me with Your spirit of love.

WOULD JESUS THINK
OF OTHERS EVEN WHEN
HE WAS IN TROUBLE?

Now there stood by the cross of Jesus his mother, and his mother's sister, Mary the wife of Cleophas, and Mary Magdalene. When Jesus therefore saw his mother, and the disciple standing by, whom he loved, he saith unto his mother, "Woman, behold thy son!" Then saith he to the disciple, "Behold thy mother!" And from that hour that disciple took her unto his own home.

JOHN 19:25–27

Dear Christ, even as You were dying, You thought about others. Help me never to be so preoccupied with my own troubles that I overlook the needs of those around me.

WOULD JESUS WORRY ABOUT HOW TO DEFEND HIMSELF AGAINST THOSE WHO THOUGHT BADLY OF HIM?

"But when they deliver you up, take no thought how or what ye shall speak: for it shall be given you in that same hour what ye shall speak. For it is not ye that speak, but the Spirit of your Father which speaketh in you."

MATTHEW 10:19–20

Hearken unto me, ye that know righteousness, the people in whose heart is my law; fear ye not the reproach of men, neither be ye afraid of their revilings.

ISAIAH 51:7

Thank You, Jesus, that I don't need to worry about defending myself. It's all in Your hands.

WHAT WOULD JESUS DO ABOUT FINANCIAL WORRIES?

"Therefore I say unto you, Take no thought for your life, what ye shall eat, or what ye shall drink; nor yet for your body, what ye shall put on. Is not the life more than meat, and the body than raiment? Behold the fowls of the air: for they sow not, neither do they reap, nor gather into barns; yet your heavenly Father feedeth them. Are ye not much better than they? Which of you by taking thought can add one cubit unto his stature? And why take ye thought for raiment? Consider the lilies of the field, how they grow; they toil not, neither do they spin: And yet I say unto you, That even Solomon in all his glory was not arrayed like one of these. Wherefore, if God so clothe the grass of the field, which to day is, and to morrow is cast into the oven, shall he not much more clothe you, O ye of little faith? Therefore take no thought, saying, What shall we eat? or, What shall we drink? or, Wherewithal shall we be clothed? (For after all these things do the Gentiles seek:) for your heavenly Father knoweth that ye have need of all these things. But seek ye first the kingdom of God, and his righteousness; and all these things shall be added unto you. Take therefore no thought for the morrow: for the morrow shall take thought for the things of itself. Sufficient unto the day is the evil thereof."

MATTHEW 6:25–34

We live under the illusion
that if we can acquire
complete control,
we can understand God. . . .
But the only way we can brush
against the hem of the Lord. . .
is to have the courage,
the faith,
to abandon control.

MADELEINE L'ENGLE

Casting all your care upon him; for he careth for you.

1 PETER 5:7

And the LORD shall guide thee continually, and satisfy thy soul in drought, and make fat thy bones: and thou shalt be like a watered garden, and like a spring of water, whose waters fail not.

ISAIAH 58:11

```
     I trust in the
    same powerful God,
  that his holy arm and power
  will carry me through. . . .
    I know his faithfulness
        and goodness,
  and I have experienced his Love.
```

MARGARET FELL FOX

And God is able to make all grace abound toward you; that ye, always having all sufficiency in all things, may abound to every good work.

2 CORINTHIANS 9:8

If You have control of my life, Lord, then I have nothing to worry about.

How would Jesus react if people called Him names and accused Him of evil?

"If they have called the master of the house Beelzebub, how much more shall they call them of his household? Fear them not therefore: for there is nothing covered, that shall not be revealed; and hid, that shall not be known."

MATTHEW 10:25–26

"Blessed are ye, when men shall hate you, and when they shall separate you from their company, and shall reproach you, and cast out your name as evil, for the Son of man's sake. Rejoice ye in that day, and leap for joy: for, behold, your reward is great in heaven: for in the like manner did their fathers unto the prophets."

LUKE 6:22–23

"Blessed are they which are persecuted for righteousness' sake: for theirs is the kingdom of heaven."

MATTHEW 5:10

Hearken unto me, ye that know righteousness, the people in whose heart is my law; fear ye not the reproach of men, neither be ye afraid of their revilings.

ISAIAH 51:7

"Then shall they deliver you up to be afflicted, and shall kill you: and ye shall be hated of all nations for my name's sake. And then shall many be offended, and shall betray one another, and shall hate one another. And many false prophets shall rise, and shall deceive many. And because iniquity shall abound, the love of many shall wax cold. But he that shall endure unto the end, the same shall be saved."

MATTHEW 24:9–13

Remind me, Lord Jesus, that what others think of me isn't important. So long as I am in right relation with You, what the world thinks isn't important.

WOULD JESUS BE
AFRAID OF
HIS ENEMIES?

"And I say unto you my friends, Be not afraid of them that kill the body, and after that have no more that they can do. But I will forewarn you whom ye shall fear: Fear him, which after he hath killed hath power to cast into hell; yea, I say unto you, Fear him."

LUKE 12:4–5

And when I saw him, I fell at his feet as dead. And he laid his right hand upon me, saying unto me, "Fear not; I am the first and the last."

REVELATION 1:17

Say to them that are of a fearful heart, Be strong, fear not: behold, your God will come with vengeance, even God with a recompence; he will come and save you.

ISAIAH 35:4

"And fear not them which kill the body, but are not able to kill the soul."

MATTHEW 10:28

For I the LORD thy God will hold thy right hand, saying unto thee, Fear not; I will help thee.

ISAIAH 41:13

No, I will not retire,
if by shedding my blood
I can promote peace,
why should I fly,
now that the honour of Christ,
and the peace of his spouse,
are in peril?

CATHERINE OF SIENA

That he would grant unto us, that we, being delivered out of the hand of our enemies, might serve him without fear.

LUKE 1:74

That we should be saved from our enemies, and from the hand of all that hate us.

LUKE 1:71

I am growing more and
more anxious that my life
may be given without
reserve to God's service. . . .
We must have a great deal
of courage and
honest conviction.

Helen Barret Montgomery

So that we may boldly say, The Lord is my helper, and I will not fear what man shall do unto me.

HEBREWS 13:6

Take the fear I feel sometimes, Jesus. I give it to You. Don't let it get in the way of my service to You.

WHAT WOULD JESUS DO IF HE WERE TAKEN TO COURT?

"And if any man will sue thee at the law, and take away thy coat, let him have thy cloak also. And whosoever shall compel thee to go a mile, go with him twain."

MATTHEW 5:40–41

What is the
gain or loss
of money compared with
the unsearchable riches
of eternal life
which are beyond
the reach of
speculation,
loss or change?

IN HIS STEPS

"Agree with thine adversary quickly, whiles thou art in the way with him; lest at any time the adversary deliver thee to the judge, and the judge deliver thee to the officer, and thou be cast into prison."

MATTHEW 5:25

The very fact that you have lawsuits among you means you have been completely defeated already. Why not rather be wronged? Why not rather be cheated?

1 CORINTHIANS 6:7 NIV

It's hard to "turn the other cheek," Lord. Grant me the humility to follow Your will.

What would Jesus do if His friends were arguing?

And he opened his mouth, and taught them, saying, . . . "Blessed are the peacemakers: for they shall be called the children of God."

MATTHEW 5:2, 9

And the fruit of righteousness is sown in peace of them that make peace.

JAMES 3:18

Be of one mind, live in peace; and the God of love and peace shall be with you.

2 CORINTHIANS 13:11

Deceit is in the heart of them that imagine evil: but to the counsellors of peace is joy.

PROVERBS 12:20

Depart from evil, and do good; seek peace, and pursue it.

PSALM 34:14

Lord, make me an
instrument of Your peace.
Where there is hatred,
let me sow love;
where there is injury,
pardon.

FRANCIS OF ASSISI

If it be possible, as much as lieth in you, live peaceably with all men.

ROMANS 12:18

Argument is such an ugly noise, Lord. Help me never to cause it—and help me to show others how to end it.

HOW WOULD JESUS FACE HIS OWN DEATH?

And when Jesus had cried with a loud voice, he said, "Father, into thy hands I commend my spirit": and having said thus, he gave up the ghost.

LUKE 23:46

Let us follow Jesus closer;
let us walk in His steps
where it will cost us
something more than
it is costing us now.

IN HIS STEPS

Remind me, Lord, that if I am following You, then death will only bring me into Your presence.

WHAT WOULD JESUS
SAY TO SOMEONE
WHO TRIED TO
PREDICT THE FUTURE?

And he said unto them, "It is not for you to know the times or the seasons, which the Father hath put in his own power."

ACTS 1:7

A man cannot discover anything about his future.

ECCLESIASTES 7:14 NIV

But of the times and the seasons, brethren, ye have no need that I write unto you. For yourselves know perfectly that the day of the Lord so cometh as a thief in the night.

1 THESSALONIANS 5:1–2

Since no man knows the future, who can tell him what is to come?

ECCLESIASTES 8:7 NIV

Once when we were going to the place of prayer, we were met by a slave girl who had a spirit by which she predicted the future. She earned a great deal of money for her owners by fortune-telling. This girl followed Paul and the rest of us, shouting, "These men are servants of the Most High God, who are telling you the way to be saved." She kept this up for many days. Finally Paul became so troubled that he turned around and said to the spirit, "In the name of Jesus Christ I command you to come out of her!" At that moment the spirit left her.

ACTS 16:16–18 NIV

How can we be troubled
about the future road,
since it belongs to Thee?
How can we be troubled
where it leads, since it
finally but leads us to Thee!

JOHN HENRY NEWMAN

Lord, You told us not to worry about tomorrow. Forgive us for spending so much time trying to figure out what is coming, when we know it's all in Your hands.

WHAT WOULD JESUS DO IF HE FACED SOMETHING HARD OR FRIGHTENING?

"Now is my soul troubled; and what shall I say? Father, save me from this hour: but for this cause came I unto this hour. Father, glorify thy name." Then came there a voice from heaven, saying, I have both glorified it, and will glorify it again.

JOHN 12:27–28

And he went a little farther, and fell on his face, and prayed, saying, "O my Father, if it be possible, let this cup pass from me: nevertheless not as I will, but as thou wilt."

MATTHEW 26:39

What time I am afraid, I will trust in thee. In God I will praise his word, in God I have put my trust; I will not fear what flesh can do unto me.

PSALM 56:3–4

As for me, I will call upon God; and the LORD shall save me. Evening, and morning, and at noon, will I pray, and cry aloud: and he shall hear my voice.

PSALM 55:16–17

Suffering can be overcome. . . .
What must one do?
One must submit.
Do not resist. Take it.
Be overwhelmed.
Accept it fully.
Make it part of life.
Everything in life that
we really accept
undergoes a change.

KATHERINE MANSFIELD

When hard times come, Lord, help me to desire Your will more than my own. Help me accept whatever happens, so that You can be glorified even in the midst of trouble.

WHAT WOULD JESUS DO IF HE WERE CONFRONTED BY SOMETHING THAT SEEMED IMPOSSIBLE?

And Jesus looking upon them saith, "With men it is impossible, but not with God: for with God all things are possible."

MARK 10:27

Now unto him that is able to do exceeding abundantly above all that we ask or think, according to the power that worketh in us.

EPHESIANS 3:20

The LORD God is my strength, and he will make my feet like hinds' feet, and he will make me to walk upon mine high places.

HABAKKUK 3:19

What is incredible to us, Jesus, is simple for You. Help me to remember Your awesome power.

WOULD JESUS BE AFRAID OF THE SUPERNATURAL?

And in the synagogue there was a man, which had a spirit of an unclean devil, and cried out with a loud voice, Saying, "Let us alone; what have we to do with thee, thou Jesus of Nazareth? art thou come to destroy us? I know thee who thou art; the Holy One of God." And Jesus rebuked him, saying, "Hold thy peace, and come out of him." And when the devil had thrown him in the midst, he came out of him, and hurt him not. And they were all amazed, and spake among themselves, saying, "What a word is this! for with authority and power he commandeth the unclean spirits, and they come out."

LUKE 4:33–36

And in that same hour he cured many of their infirmities and plagues, and of evil spirits; and unto many that were blind he gave sight.

LUKE 7:21

And when he had called unto him his twelve disciples, he gave them power against unclean spirits, to cast them out, and to heal all manner of sickness and all manner of disease.

MATTHEW 10:1

And Jesus rebuked him, saying, "Hold thy peace, and come out of him." And when the unclean spirit had torn him, and cried with a loud voice, he came out of him. And they were all amazed, insomuch that they questioned among themselves, saying, "What thing is this? what new doctrine is this? for with authority commandeth he even the unclean spirits, and they do obey him."

MARK 1:25–27

Lord, You've shown us that the supernatural bows to Your will. May we respect the powers of evil, but not fear them.

How would Jesus handle daily life?

"Our Father which art in heaven,
Hallowed be thy name.
Thy kingdom come.
Thy will be done,
as in heaven, so in earth."

Luke 11:2

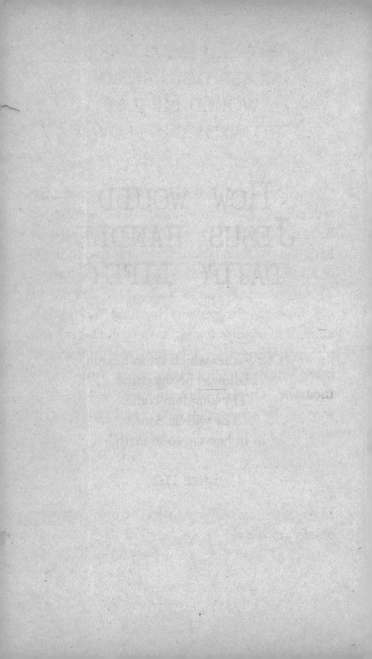

WOULD JESUS MAKE REALISTIC PLANS OR WOULD HE JUST "GO WITH THE FLOW"?

"For which of you, intending to build a tower, sitteth not down first, and counteth the cost, whether he have sufficient to finish it? Lest haply, after he hath laid the foundation, and is not able to finish it, all that behold it begin to mock him, Saying, This man began to build, and was not able to finish. Or what king, going to make war against another king, sitteth not down first, and consulteth whether he be able with ten thousand to meet him that cometh against him with twenty thousand? Or else, while the other is yet a great way off, he sendeth an ambassage, and desireth conditions of peace."

LUKE 14:28–32

Make plans by seeking advice; if you wage war, obtain guidance.

PROVERBS 20:18 NIV

It is not good to have zeal without knowledge, nor to be hasty and miss the way.

PROVERBS 19:2 NIV

The plans of the righteous are just.

PROVERBS 12:5 NIV

A prudent man gives thought to his steps.

PROVERBS 14:15 NIV

There are many
perplexing questions
in our civilization
that are not mentioned
in the teachings of Jesus.
How am I going to tell
what He would do?

IN HIS STEPS

I need Your wisdom, God. Help me to make wise plans for my life, plans that will lead me in Your steps. Please show me what You want me to do.

WHAT WOULD JESUS DO
IF SOMEONE WANTED
TO BORROW SOMETHING
FROM HIM?

"Give to him that asketh thee, and from him that would borrow of thee turn not thou away."

MATTHEW 5:42

"If you lend money to one of my people among you who is needy, do not be like a moneylender; charge him no interest."

EXODUS 22:25 NIV

"But love ye your enemies, and do good, and lend, hoping for nothing again; and your reward shall be great, and ye shall be the children of the Highest: for he is kind unto the unthankful and to the evil."

LUKE 6:35

Jesus, please help me avoid selfishness.

HOW WOULD JESUS
EVALUATE NEW IDEAS?

"Ye shall know them by their fruits. Do men gather grapes of thorns, or figs of thistles? Even so every good tree bringeth forth good fruit; but a corrupt tree bringeth forth evil fruit. A good tree cannot bring forth evil fruit, neither can a corrupt tree bring forth good fruit. Every tree that bringeth not forth good fruit is hewn down, and cast into the fire. Wherefore by their fruits ye shall know them."

MATTHEW 7:16–20

"Stop judging by mere appearances, and make a right judgment."

JOHN 7:24 NIV

Ye shall do no unrighteousness in judgment: thou shalt not respect the person of the poor, nor honour the person of the mighty: but in righteousness shalt thou judge thy neighbour.

LEVITICUS 19:15

"There is no way
that I know of,"
replied the pastor,
"except as we study
Jesus through the medium
of the Holy Spirit. . . .
There is no other test
that I know of."

IN HIS STEPS

Help me, Jesus, not to have a closed mind to new ideas. Remind me to use Your Spirit's light to illumine everything that comes into my life.

How would Jesus handle
money and possessions?

"Don't store up treasures here on earth, where they can be eaten by moths and get rusty, and where thieves break in and steal. Store your treasures in heaven. . .where they will never become moth-eaten or rusty and where they will be safe from thieves. Wherever your treasure is, there your heart and thoughts will also be."

MATTHEW 6:19–21 NLT

"No servant can serve two masters: for either he will hate the one, and love the other; or else he will hold to the one, and despise the other. Ye cannot serve God and mammon."

LUKE 16:13

But what things were gain to me, those I counted loss for Christ. Yea doubtless, and I count all things but loss for the excellency of the knowledge of Christ Jesus my Lord: for whom I have suffered the loss of all things, and do count them but dung, that I may win Christ.

PHILIPPIANS 3:7–8

Charge them that are rich in this world, that they be not highminded, nor trust in uncertain riches, but in the living God, who giveth us richly all things to enjoy; That they do good, that they be rich in good works, ready to distribute.

1 TIMOTHY 6:17–18

And he said unto them, "Take heed, and beware of covetousness: for a man's life consisteth not in the abundance of the things which he possesseth." And he spake a parable unto them, saying, "The ground of a certain rich man brought forth plentifully: And he thought within himself, saying, 'What shall I do, because I have no room where to bestow my fruits?' And he said, 'This will I do: I will pull down my barns, and build greater; and there will I bestow all my fruits and my goods. And I will say to my soul, Soul, thou hast much goods laid up for many years; take thine ease, eat, drink, and be merry.' But God said unto him, 'Thou fool, this night thy soul shall be required of thee: then whose shall those things be, which thou hast provided?' So is he that layeth up treasure for himself, and is not rich toward God."

LUKE 12:15–21

He that loveth silver shall not be satisfied with silver; nor he that loveth abundance with increase: this is also vanity.

ECCLESIASTES 5:10

I have come to know lately that
the money which I have called
my own is not mine, but God's.
If I, as a steward of His,
see some wise way to
invest His money,
it is not an occasion
for vainglory or thanks
from anyone simply because
I have proved honest in
my administration of
the funds He has asked me
to use for His glory.

IN HIS STEPS

For wisdom is a defence, and money is a defence: but the excellency of knowledge is, that wisdom giveth life to them that have it.

ECCLESIASTES 7:12

Wherefore do ye spend money for that which is not bread? and your labour for that which satisfieth not?

ISAIAH 55:2

It is not the rich man only who
is under the domination of things;
they too are slaves who,
having no money,
are unhappy from the lack of it.

GEORGE MACDONALD

For the love of money is the root of all evil: which while some coveted after, they have erred from the faith, and pierced themselves through with many sorrows.

1 TIMOTHY 6:10

Dear God, help me not to take pride in money. Help me not to worry about it either. Instead, remind me that my money and all I own now belong to You.

WOULD JESUS, WHEN HE WAS A GUEST, TAKE WHATEVER HE WAS SERVED?

"Stay in that house, eating and drinking whatever they give you. . . . When you enter a town and are welcomed, eat what is set before you."

LUKE 10:7–8 NIV

Remind me to follow You, Jesus, even in small things—like being gracious to my hosts and eating what I am served. Let me never forget that I represent You.

WOULD JESUS SWEAR?

"Again, ye have heard that it hath been said by them of old time, Thou shalt not forswear thyself, but shalt perform unto the Lord thine oaths: But I say unto you, Swear not at all; neither by heaven; for it is God's throne: Nor by the earth; for it is his footstool: neither by Jerusalem; for it is the city of the great King. Neither shalt thou swear by thy head, because thou canst not make one hair white or black. But let your communication be, Yea, yea; Nay, nay: for whatsoever is more than these cometh of evil."

MATTHEW 5:33–37

Let no corrupt communication proceed out of your mouth, but that which is good to the use of edifying, that it may minister grace unto the hearers.

EPHESIANS 4:29

Let my conversation, Lord Jesus, always please You.

HOW WOULD JESUS HANDLE EMOTIONS?

Above all else,
guard your heart,
for it is the wellspring of life.

PROVERBS 4:23 NIV

WHAT WOULD JESUS
DO WHEN HE WAS HAPPY?

In that hour Jesus rejoiced in spirit and said, "I thank thee, O Father, Lord of heaven and earth."

LUKE 10:21

"Rejoice ye in that day, and leap for joy."

LUKE 6:23

But let all those that put their trust in thee rejoice: let them ever shout for joy, because thou defendest them: let them also that love thy name be joyful in thee.

PSALM 5:11

Yet believing, ye rejoice with joy unspeakable and full of glory.

1 PETER 1:8

I will be glad and rejoice in thee: I will sing praise to thy name, O thou most High.

PSALM 9:2

And Mary said, "My soul doth magnify the Lord, And my spirit hath rejoiced in God my Saviour. For he hath regarded the low estate of his handmaiden: for, behold, from henceforth all generations shall call me blessed. For he that is mighty hath done to me great things; and holy is his name."

LUKE 1:46–49

Now thank we all our God,
With hearts and hands and voices
Who wondrous things hath done
in whom his world rejoices.

CATHERINE WINKWORTH

O satisfy us early with thy mercy; that we may rejoice and be glad all our days.

PSALM 90:14

Make a joyful noise unto God, all ye lands: Sing forth the honour of his name: make his praise glorious.

PSALM 66:1–2

And now shall mine head be lifted up above mine
enemies round about me: therefore will I offer in
his tabernacle sacrifices of joy; I will sing, yea, I
will sing praises unto the Lord.

PSALM 27:6

My song shall be of Jesus,
when sitting at his feet,
I call to mind his goodness
and know my joy's complete.

FANNY J. CROSBY

---

*When I'm sad or in trouble, Father, I'm quick to turn
to You—but sometimes when I'm happy, I forget You.
Remind me to give You my joy, as well as my sorrow
and fear. Let me never forget that You are the source
of all my happiness.*

WHAT WOULD JESUS SAY IS THE RIGHT WAY TO HANDLE ANGER?

"You have heard that the law of Moses says, 'Do not murder. If you commit murder, you are subject to judgment.' But I say, if you are angry with someone, you are subject to judgment! If you say to your friend, 'You idiot,' you are in danger of being brought before the court. And if you curse someone, you are in danger of the fires of hell.

"So if you are standing before the altar in the Temple, offering a sacrifice to God, and you suddenly remember that someone has something against you, leave your sacrifice there beside the altar. Go and be reconciled to that person. Then come and offer your sacrifice to God."

MATTHEW 5:21–24 NLT

"And when ye stand praying, forgive, if ye have ought against any: that your Father also which is in heaven may forgive you your trespasses."

MARK 11:25

A fool gives full vent to anger, but a wise person quietly holds it back.

PROVERBS 29:11 NLT

He that is slow to anger is better than the mighty; and he that ruleth his spirit than he that taketh a city.

PROVERBS 16:32

Injuries quickly forgotten
quickly pass away. . . .
"Love thy neighbor"
is a precept which could
transform the world if it
were universally practiced.

MARY McLEOD BETHUNE

Oh my lord, let thy servant, I pray thee, speak a word in my lord's ears, and let not thine anger burn against thy servant.

GENESIS 44:18

So that contrariwise ye ought rather to forgive him, and comfort him, lest perhaps such a one should be swallowed up with overmuch sorrow. . . . To whom ye forgive any thing, I forgive also: for if I forgave any thing, to whom I forgave it, for your sakes forgave I it in the person of Christ.

2 CORINTHIANS 2:7, 10

Cease from anger, and forsake wrath: fret not thyself in any wise to do evil.

PSALM 37:8

Dear Jesus, Your Word makes clear that I cannot be close to You if I allow anger to come between me and another person. Take my angry feelings, Lord, and transform them with Your love. Give me the strength to forgive.

What would Jesus do if He were looking at someone who was physically attractive?

"Ye have heard that it was said by them of old time, Thou shalt not commit adultery: But I say unto you, That whosoever looketh on a woman to lust after her hath committed adultery with her already in his heart."

MATTHEW 5:27–28

God wants you to be holy, so you should keep clear of all sexual sin. Then each of you will control your body and live in holiness and honor—not in lustful passion.

1 THESSALONIANS 4:3–5 NLT

Then when lust hath conceived, it bringeth forth sin: and sin, when it is finished, bringeth forth death.

JAMES 1:15

Lust not after her beauty in thine heart; neither let her take thee with her eyelids.

PROVERBS 6:25

Now concerning the things whereof ye wrote unto me: It is good for a man not to touch a woman. Nevertheless, to avoid fornication, let every man have his own wife, and let every woman have her own husband.

1 CORINTHIANS 7:1–2

This I say then, Walk in the Spirit, and ye shall not fulfil the lust of the flesh. . . . Now the works of the flesh are manifest, which are these; Adultery, fornication, uncleanness, lasciviousness.

GALATIANS 5:16, 19

Help me, Christ, to never look at another person as an object to be desired. Remind me that You are as concerned with my internal thoughts as You are with my external actions.

WHAT WOULD JESUS DO IF HIS FRIENDS WERE SAD?

When Jesus saw her weeping, and the Jews who had come along with her also weeping, he was deeply moved in spirit and troubled. Jesus wept.

JOHN 11:33, 35 NIV

"These things I have spoken unto you, that in me ye might have peace. In the world ye shall have tribulation: but be of good cheer; I have overcome the world."

JOHN 16:33

Thou wilt shew me the path of life: in thy presence is fulness of joy; at thy right hand there are pleasures for evermore.

PSALM 16:11

Weeping may endure for a night, but joy cometh in the morning.

PSALM 30:5

That ye might walk worthy of the Lord unto all pleasing, being fruitful in every good work, and increasing in the knowledge of God; Strengthened with all might, according to his glorious power, unto all patience and longsuffering with joyfulness.

COLOSSIANS 1:10–11

What our churches need
today more than anything else
is this factor of
joyful suffering for Jesus
in some form.
Suffering that
does not eliminate,
but does appear to intensify,
a positive and practical joy.

IN HIS STEPS

Help me, Lord, to find You even in the midst of sadness. Take my sorrow and in its place give me a positive, practical joy.

WOULD JESUS NEED TO
SPEND TIME ALONE?

When Jesus heard of it, he departed thence by ship into a desert place apart: and when the people had heard thereof, they followed him on foot out of the cities.

MATTHEW 14:13

And in the morning, rising up a great while before day, he went out, and departed into a solitary place, and there prayed.

MARK 1:35

And when he had sent the multitudes away, he went up into a mountain apart to pray: and when the evening was come, he was there alone.

MATTHEW 14:23

Now when Jesus saw great multitudes about him, he gave commandment to depart unto the other side.

MATTHEW 8:18

And he said unto them, "Come ye yourselves apart into a desert place, and rest a while": for there were many coming and going, and they had no leisure so much as to eat. And they departed into a desert place by ship privately.

MARK 6:31–32

And when he had sent them away, he departed into a mountain to pray.

MARK 6:46

And Jesus being full of the Holy Ghost returned from Jordan, and was led by the Spirit into the wilderness.

LUKE 4:1

And it came to pass in those days, that he went out into a mountain to pray, and continued all night in prayer to God.

LUKE 6:12

And I said, Oh that I had wings like a dove! for then would I fly away, and be at rest.

PSALM 55:6

Deserts, silence, solitudes
are not necessarily places
but states of mind and heart.
These deserts can be found
in the midst of the city,
and in the every day
of our lives. . . .
They will be small solitudes,
little deserts,
tiny pools of silence,
but the experience
they will bring,
if we are disposed
to enter them,
may be as exultant
and as holy as all the
deserts in the world.

CATHERINE DE HUECK DOHERTY

He maketh me to lie down in green pastures: he
leadeth me beside the still waters. He restoreth
my soul.

PSALM 23:2–3

Therefore, behold, I will allure her, and bring her into the wilderness, and speak comfortably unto her.

HOSEA 2:14

When Jesus therefore perceived that they would come and take him by force, to make him a king, he departed again into a mountain himself alone.

JOHN 6:15

The wilderness and the solitary place shall be glad for them; and the desert shall rejoice, and blossom as the rose.

ISAIAH 35:1

Remind me, Jesus, to take time to be alone with You.

WHAT WOULD JESUS SAY TO SOMEONE WHO WAS OBSESSED WITH FOOD?

But he said unto them, "I have meat to eat that ye know not of. . ." Jesus saith unto them, "My meat is to do the will of him that sent me, and to finish his work."

JOHN 4:32, 34

"I am the living bread which came down from heaven: if any man eat of this bread, he shall live for ever: and the bread that I will give is my flesh, which I will give for the life of the world."

JOHN 6:51

Hearken diligently unto me, and eat ye that which is good, and let your soul delight itself in fatness.

ISAIAH 55:2

"It is written, Man shall not live by bread alone, but by every word that proceedeth out of the mouth of God."

MATTHEW 4:4

Then Jesus said unto them, "Verily, verily, I say unto you, Moses gave you not that bread from heaven; but my Father giveth you the true bread from heaven. For the bread of God is he which cometh down from heaven, and giveth life unto the world." Then said they unto him, "Lord, evermore give us this bread." And Jesus said unto them, "I am the bread of life: he that cometh to me shall never hunger; and he that believeth on me shall never thirst."

JOHN 6:32–35

When I am tempted to turn to food—or anything else—for comfort, trying to fill the neediness inside me, remind me that You, Lord, are the only true nourishment for my heart. Only You can satisfy my soul.

WHAT WOULD JESUS SAY
IF THOSE AROUND HIM
WERE FRIGHTENED?

But straightway Jesus spake unto them, saying, "Be of good cheer; it is I; be not afraid."

MATTHEW 14:27

"Peace I leave with you, my peace I give unto you: not as the world giveth, give I unto you. Let not your heart be troubled, neither let it be afraid."

JOHN 14:27

As soon as Jesus heard the word that was spoken, he saith unto the ruler of the synagogue, "Be not afraid, only believe."

MARK 5:36

For they all saw him, and were troubled. And immediately he talked with them, and saith unto them, "Be of good cheer: it is I; be not afraid."

MARK 6:50

The LORD is my light and my salvation; whom shall I fear? the LORD is the strength of my life; of whom shall I be afraid?

PSALM 27:1

```
       I am well.
     All is well,
     well forever.
        I see,
 wherever I turn my eyes,
 whether I live or die,
   nothing but victory.
```

LADY HUNTINGDON

In God have I put my trust: I will not be afraid what man can do unto me.

PSALM 56:11

And Jesus came and touched them, and said, "Arise, and be not afraid."

MATTHEW 17:7

Be strong and of a good courage: for. . .I will be with thee.

DEUTERONOMY 31:23

Then spake the Lord to Paul in the night by a vision, "Be not afraid, but speak, and hold not thy peace: For I am with thee, and no man shall set on thee to hurt thee: for I have much people in this city."

ACTS 18:9–10

What time I am afraid, I will trust in thee. In God I will praise his word, in God I have put my trust; I will not fear what flesh can do unto me.

PSALM 56:3–4

Thank You, Lord, that when I'm scared, Your Spirit is always close beside me. Help me spread Your comfort when those around me are frightened.

How would Jesus treat people who were minorities or different in some way?

There cometh a woman
of Samaria to draw water:
Jesus saith unto her,
"Give me to drink."
Then saith the woman of Samaria unto him,
"How is it that thou, being a Jew,
askest drink of me,
which am a woman of Samaria?
for the Jews have no dealings
with the Samaritans."

JOHN 4:7, 9

WHAT WOULD JESUS DO IF HE FOUND SOMEONE IN TROUBLE WHO WAS FROM A DIFFERENT RACE OR RELIGION?

I should preach among the Gentiles the unsearchable riches of Christ.

EPHESIANS 3:8

For the LORD your God is God of gods, and Lord of lords, a great God, a mighty, and a terrible, which regardeth not persons, nor taketh reward: He. . .loveth the stranger, in giving him food and raiment. Love ye therefore the stranger: for ye were strangers in the land of Egypt.

DEUTERONOMY 10:17–19

Thou shalt neither vex a stranger, nor oppress him: for ye were strangers in the land of Egypt.

EXODUS 22:21

Jesus. . .said, "A certain man went down from Jerusalem to Jericho, and fell among thieves, which stripped him of his raiment, and wounded him, and departed, leaving him half dead. And by chance there came down a certain priest that way: and when he saw him, he passed by on the other side. And likewise a Levite, when he was at the place, came and looked on him, and passed by on the other side. But a certain Samaritan, as he journeyed, came where he was: and when he saw him, he had compassion on him, And went to him, and bound up his wounds, pouring in oil and wine, and set him on his own beast, and brought him to an inn, and took care of him. And on the morrow when he departed, he took out two pence, and gave them to the host, and said unto him, Take care of him; and whatsoever thou spendest more, when I come again, I will repay thee. Which now of these three, thinkest thou, was neighbour unto him that fell among the thieves?" And he said, "He that shewed mercy on him." Then said Jesus unto him, "Go, and do thou likewise."

LUKE 10:30–37

Also thou shalt not oppress a stranger: for ye know the heart of a stranger.

EXODUS 23:9

Christ has no body now
on earth but yours;
yours are the only hands
with which He can do His work,
yours are the only feet
with which He can
go about the world,
yours are the only eyes
through which His compassion
can shine forth upon
a troubled world.
Christ has no body
on earth now but yours.

TERESA OF AVILA

Do not forget to entertain strangers, for by so doing some people have entertained angels without knowing it.

HEBREWS 13:2 NIV

Show me any prejudice that hides in my life, God. Let me never forget that we are all Your children.

WOULD JESUS HAVE NOTICED EVEN INSIGNIFICANT PEOPLE?

And, behold, there was a man named Zacchaeus, which was the chief among the publicans, and he was rich. And he sought to see Jesus who he was; and could not for the press, because he was little of stature. And he ran before, and climbed up into a sycamore tree to see him: for he was to pass that way.

And when Jesus came to the place, he looked up, and saw him, and said unto him, "Zacchaeus, make haste, and come down; for to day I must abide at thy house." And he made haste, and came down, and received him joyfully.

LUKE 19:2–6

"When you give a banquet, invite the poor, the crippled, the lame, the blind, and you will be blessed. Although they cannot repay you, you will be repaid at the resurrection of the righteous."

LUKE 14:13–14 NIV

He will regard the prayer of the destitute, and not despise their prayer.

PSALM 102:17

What would Jesus do
about the great army of
unemployed and desperate
who tramp the streets. . . ?
Would Jesus . . .
say that it was
none of His business?

IN HIS STEPS

Love ye therefore the stranger: for ye were strangers in the land of Egypt.

DEUTERONOMY 10:19

Remind me, God, what my business here on earth really is.

HOW DID
JESUS TREAT WOMEN?

And he arose out of the synagogue, and entered into Simon's house. And Simon's wife's mother was taken with a great fever; and they besought him for her. And he stood over her, and rebuked the fever; and it left her: and immediately she arose and ministered unto them.

LUKE 4:38–39

Now when he came nigh to the gate of the city, behold, there was a dead man carried out, the only son of his mother, and she was a widow: and much people of the city was with her. And when the Lord saw her, he had compassion on her.

LUKE 7:12–13

So you are all children of God through faith in Christ Jesus. There is no longer Jew or Gentile, slave or free, male or female. For you are all Christians—you are one in Christ Jesus.

GALATIANS 3:26, 28 NLT

And a woman having an issue of blood twelve years, which had spent all her living upon physicians, neither could be healed of any, Came behind him, and touched the border of his garment: and immediately her issue of blood stanched. And Jesus said, "Who touched me?" When all denied, Peter and they that were with him said, "Master, the multitude throng thee and press thee, and sayest thou, 'Who touched me?'" And Jesus said, "Somebody hath touched me: for I perceive that virtue is gone out of me."

And when the woman saw that she was not hid, she came trembling, and falling down before him, she declared unto him before all the people for what cause she had touched him, and how she was healed immediately. And he said unto her, "Daughter, be of good comfort: thy faith hath made thee whole; go in peace."

LUKE 8:43–48

When we ignore large segments
of the body of Christ
we are quenching
the Holy Spirit.

KARI TORJESEN MALCOLM

And, behold, a woman in the city, which was a sinner, when she knew that Jesus sat at meat in the Pharisee's house, brought an alabaster box of ointment, And stood at his feet behind him weeping, and began to wash his feet with tears, and did wipe them with the hairs of her head, and kissed his feet, and anointed them with the ointment.

Now when the Pharisee which had bidden him saw it, he spake within himself, saying, "This man, if he were a prophet, would have known who and what manner of woman this is that toucheth him: for she is a sinner." And Jesus answering . . . said unto Simon, "Seest thou this woman? I entered into thine house, thou gavest me no water for my feet: but she hath washed my feet with tears, and wiped them with the hairs of her head. Thou gavest me no kiss: but this woman since the time I came in hath not ceased to kiss my feet. My head with oil thou didst not anoint: but this woman hath anointed my feet with ointment. Wherefore I say unto thee, Her sins, which are many, are forgiven; for she loved much: but to whom little is forgiven, the same loveth little."

And he said unto her, "Thy sins are forgiven." And they that sat at meat with him began to say within themselves, "Who is this that forgiveth sins also?" And he said to the woman, "Thy faith hath saved thee; go in peace."

LUKE 7:37–40, 44–50

And the scribes and Pharisees brought unto him a woman taken in adultery; and when they had set her in the midst, They say unto him, "Master, this woman was taken in adultery, in the very act. Now Moses in the law commanded us, that such should be stoned: but what sayest thou?" This they said, tempting him, that they might have to accuse him. But Jesus stooped down, and with his finger wrote on the ground, as though he heard them not. So when they continued asking him, he lifted up himself, and said unto them, "He that is without sin among you, let him first cast a stone at her." And again he stooped down, and wrote on the ground.

And they which heard it, being convicted by their own conscience, went out one by one, beginning at the eldest, even unto the last: and Jesus was left alone, and the woman standing in the midst. When Jesus had lifted up himself, and saw none but the woman, he said unto her, "Woman, where are those thine accusers? hath no man condemned thee?" She said, "No man, Lord." And Jesus said unto her, "Neither do I condemn thee: go, and sin no more."

JOHN 8:3–11

Perhaps it is no wonder
that women were first
at the Cradle and
last at the Cross.
They had never known
a man like this Man—
there never has been such another.
A prophet and teacher who
never nagged at them,
never flattered or coaxed
or patronised;
who rebuked without querulousness
and praised without condescension;
who took their questions
and their arguments seriously;
who never mapped out
their sphere for them.

DOROTHY L. SAYERS

And, behold, there was a woman which had a spirit of infirmity eighteen years, and was bowed together, and could in no wise lift up herself. And when Jesus saw her, he called her to him, and said unto her, "Woman, thou art loosed from thine infirmity." And he laid his hands on her: and immediately she was made straight, and glorified God.

LUKE 13:11–13

There cometh a woman of Samaria to draw water: Jesus saith unto her, "Give me to drink. . . ." Then saith the woman of Samaria unto him, "How is it that thou, being a Jew, askest drink of me, which am a woman of Samaria? for the Jews have no dealings with the Samaritans." Jesus answered and said unto her, "If thou knewest the gift of God, and who it is that saith to thee, Give me to drink; thou wouldest have asked of him, and he would have given thee living water. . . ." And upon this came his disciples, and marvelled that he talked with the woman: yet no man said, "What seekest thou? or, Why talkest thou with her?"

JOHN 4:7, 9–10, 27

In a time and place where women were second-class citizens, Lord, You showed us by Your actions that we are all equally loved.

How would Jesus relate to the church?

The church,
Which is his body,
the fulness of him that
filleth all in all.

Ephesians 1:22–23

WOULD JESUS THINK IT WAS IMPORTANT TO OBEY LOTS OF RULES IN ORDER TO BE "CHRISTIAN"?

"Teacher, which is the greatest commandment in the Law?"

Jesus replied: " 'Love the Lord your God with all your heart and with all your soul and with all your mind.' This is the first and greatest commandment. And the second is like it: 'Love your neighbor as yourself.' All the Law and the Prophets hang on these two commandments."

MATTHEW 22:36–40 NIV

And as he spake, a certain Pharisee besought him to dine with him: and he went in, and sat down to meat. And when the Pharisee saw it, he marvelled that he had not first washed before dinner. And the Lord said unto him, "Now do ye Pharisees make clean the outside of the cup and the platter; but your inward part is full of ravening and wickedness. Ye fools, did not he that made that which is without make that which is within also?"

LUKE 11:37–40

Indignant because Jesus had healed on the Sabbath, the synagogue ruler said to the people, "There are six days for work. So come and be healed on those days, not on the Sabbath." The Lord answered him, "You hypocrites! Doesn't each of you on the Sabbath untie his ox or donkey from the stall and lead it out to give it water? Then should not this woman, a daughter of Abraham, who Satan has kept bound for eighteen long years, be set free on the Sabbath day from what bound her?"

LUKE 13:14–16 NIV

The Church must. . .
not put unbiblical barriers
before (people) to make their
turning more difficult
or impossible. At the same time,
she must put clearly before them
the biblical conditions
for becoming Christians.

B. V. SUBBAMMA

Keep my eyes on You, Jesus, rather than on any human institution, even the Church.

WHAT WOULD JESUS DO IF HE MET SOMEONE WHO CLAIMED TO BE A CHRISTIAN AND YET ACTED DIFFERENTLY THAN HIS OTHER FOLLOWERS?

And John answered him, saying, "Master, we saw one casting out devils in thy name, and he followeth not us: and we forbad him, because he followeth not us." But Jesus said, "Forbid him not: for there is no man which shall do a miracle in my name, that can lightly speak evil of me. For he that is not against us is on our part. For whosoever shall give you a cup of water to drink in my name, because ye belong to Christ, verily I say unto you, he shall not lose his reward."

MARK 9:38–41

Help me to realize, Jesus, that not every Christian will be just like me. Help me to enjoy the variety of individuals in Your family.

Would Jesus rigidly obey religious laws? Would He think strict obedience makes a person "good"?

"Woe unto you, scribes and Pharisees, hypocrites! for ye pay tithe of mint and anise and cummin, and have omitted the weightier matters of the law, judgment, mercy, and faith: these ought ye to have done, and not to leave the other undone.

"Ye blind guides, which strain at a gnat, and swallow a camel. Woe unto you, scribes and Pharisees, hypocrites! for ye make clean the outside of the cup and of the platter, but within they are full of extortion and excess. Thou blind Pharisee, cleanse first that which is within the cup and platter, that the outside of them may be clean also. Woe unto you, scribes and Pharisees, hypocrites! for ye are like unto whited sepulchres, which indeed appear beautiful outward, but are within full of dead men's bones, and of all uncleanness. Even so ye also outwardly appear righteous unto men, but within ye are full of hypocrisy and iniquity."

MATTHEW 23:23–28

"Are you still so dull?" Jesus asked them. "Don't you see that whatever enters the mouth goes into the stomach and then out of the body? But the things that come out of the mouth come from the heart, and these make a man 'unclean.' For out of the heart come evil thoughts, murder, adultery, sexual immorality, theft, false testimony, slander. These are what make a man 'unclean'; but eating with unwashed hands does not make him 'unclean.' "

MATTHEW 15:16–20 (NIV)

The heart of Religion is not
an opinion about God. . .
it is a personal relationship
with God.

WILLIAM TEMPLE

At that time Jesus went on the sabbath day through the corn; and his disciples were an hunge red, and began to pluck the ears of corn, and to eat. But when the Pharisees saw it, they said unto him, "Behold, thy disciples do that which is not lawful to do upon the sabbath day." But he said unto them, "Have ye not read what David did, when he was an hungred, and they that were with him; How he entered into the house of God, and did eat the shewbread, which was not lawful for him to eat, neither for them which were with him, but only for the priests? Or have ye not read in the law, how that on the sabbath days the priests in the temple profane the sabbath, and are blameless? But I say unto you, That in this place is one greater than the temple. But if ye had known what this meaneth, I will have mercy, and not sacrifice, ye would not have condemned the guiltless. For the Son of man is Lord even of the sabbath day."

And when he was departed thence, he went into their synagogue: And, behold, there was a man which had his hand withered. And they asked him, saying, "Is it lawful to heal on the sabbath days?" that they might accuse him. And he said unto them, "What man shall there be among you, that shall have one sheep, and if it fall into a pit on the sabbath day, will he not lay hold on it, and lift it out? How much then is a man better than a sheep? Wherefore it is lawful to do well on the sabbath days." Then saith he to the man, "Stretch forth thine hand." And he stretched it forth; and it was restored whole, like as the other.

MATTHEW 12:1–13

Although most of the many people who came from Ephraim, Manasseh, Issachar and Zebulun had not purified themselves, yet they ate the Passover, contrary to what was written. But Hezekiah prayed for them, saying, "May the LORD, who is good, pardon everyone who sets his heart on seeking God—the LORD, the God of his fathers—even if he is not clean according to the rules of the sanctuary." And the LORD heard Hezekiah and healed the people.

2 CHRONICLES 30:18–20 NIV

When religion goes wrong
it is because,
in one form or another,
men have made the mistake
of trying to turn to God
without turning away
from the self.

AELRED GRAHAM

Jesus, remind me that religious rules are empty and meaningless without Your love.

Would Jesus
Attend Church?

And he came to Nazareth, where he had been brought up: and, as his custom was, he went into the synagogue on the sabbath day, and stood up for to read.

LUKE 4:16

You are not alone,
you are in the Church. . . .
In that community
you are sheltered and
united with all those
all over the world
who believe in Christ.

HANS KUNG

Thank You, Jesus, for Your body, the church.

How would Jesus relate to the government and people in power?

And he sat down,
and called the twelve,
and saith unto them,
"If any man desire to be first,
the same shall be last of all,
and servant of all."

Mark 9:35

WOULD JESUS PAY TAXES?

And when they were come to Capernaum, they that received tribute money came to Peter, and said, "Doth not your master pay tribute?" He saith, "Yes." And when he was come into the house, Jesus prevented him, saying, "What thinkest thou, Simon? of whom do the kings of the earth take custom or tribute? of their own children, or of strangers?" Peter saith unto him, "Of strangers." Jesus saith unto him, "Then are the children free. Notwithstanding, lest we should offend them, go thou to the sea, and cast an hook, and take up the fish that first cometh up; and when thou hast opened his mouth, thou shalt find a piece of money: that take, and give unto them for me and thee."

MATTHEW 17:24–27

And they brought unto him a penny. And he saith unto them, "Whose is this image and super-scription?" They say unto him, "Caesar's." Then saith he unto them, "Render therefore unto Caesar the things which are Caesar's; and unto God the things that are God's."

MATTHEW 22:19–21

I might not enjoy it, Lord, but help me to pay my taxes—as You have set the example.

DID JESUS WORRY ABOUT OFFENDING THE PEOPLE WHO HAD PRESTIGE AND POWER?

Then came his disciples, and said unto him, "Knowest thou that the Pharisees were offended, after they heard this saying?" But he answered and said, "Every plant, which my heavenly Father hath not planted, shall be rooted up. Let them alone: they be blind leaders of the blind. And if the blind lead the blind, both shall fall into the ditch."

MATTHEW 15:12–14

And Jesus went into the temple of God, and cast out all them that sold and bought in the temple, and overthrew the tables of the moneychangers, and the seats of them that sold doves.

MATTHEW 21:12

I don't want to be obnoxious, Jesus, but help me always to speak Your truth—no matter who disagrees.